Horace
and the
Ghost Dog

SALLY MAGNUSSON

Illustrated by Norman Stone

BLACK & WHITE PUBLISHING

First published 2013
by Black & White Publishing Ltd
29 Ocean Drive, Edinburgh EH6 6JL

1 3 5 7 9 10 8 6 4 2   13 14 15 16

ISBN: 978 1 84502 638 7

ALBA | CHRUTHACHAIL

Typeset by Richard Budd Design
Reprografics by syntax21.co.uk
Printed and bound in Poland by
www.hussarbooks.pl

A SECRET MESSAGE
FOR READERS

Ask a grown-up 'What is a haggis?' and this is
what they will tell you.

A haggis, they will say, is a dish made from
the mashed insides of a sheep. Scots like eating it
on the birthday of their great poet, Robert Burns,
who wrote a poem about how it gushes out of the
bag like a warm, wet pudding.

Yes, I know. Yuk.

But what would you say if I told you that
the haggis is an animal belonging to a species
as ancient as the unicorn, or the centaur, or the
mighty griffin? Only smaller and fatter and, let's
face it, not so mighty.

What would you say if I told you that greedy
haggis hunters have snatched so many haggises to
boil for dinner that there are only a few left on
the face of the earth?

Perhaps you can imagine what it would feel like to be a lone haggis on the run from those hunters. He would need friends, wouldn't he? He would need animals to protect him, but also human friends to keep his whereabouts secret from the enemy. He would need you.

So, let the grown-ups believe their own story if they want to. I am going to tell you a better one. And once you have read it, please remember to keep our secret safe – or this timid endangered species may be lost forever.

The Author

1

The Cat's visitors padded into the dingy barn. It was cold. Everyone looked grumpy.

'So why have you dragged us all here?' demanded a lean figure, draping himself across a bale of hay. 'Funny time for a social visit.'

'This is not a social visit, Skull,' snapped The Cat With No Name. 'It's a planning meeting.'

'We know all about your plans,' spat another, sharpening his claws on a grinding stone. 'Remember the Great Mouse Hunt, everyone?'

The Cat shifted uncomfortably.

'OK, Fang, but how was I to know it was the mice's annual outing to Cheddar Gorge? At least you caught something, Needletooth.'

'One mangy vole and a leathery old ferret,' muttered Needletooth gloomily, spitting out a

1

fishbone. 'Not what I was promised.'

The Cat looked flustered. 'Well, this is different. This is bigger prey than a mouse, my friends. My master has put a reward on this creature's head and, believe me, it will be worth your while.'

Skull fixed her with a mean look. 'I don't work for rewards,' he hissed. 'I work for meat.'

'Oh, you'll get plenty of that, Skull, I assure you,' the Cat smirked. 'Our prey is extremely well padded. Not unlike . . .' Her eyes drifted to a podgy white cat chomping happily on a marshmallow.

'I find that remark extremely offensive,' retorted the marshmallow eater, swallowing quickly. 'Just because my mistress likes to look after me well.'

'Well, I hope you're up to the effort tonight, Diddums,' replied the Cat. 'This is a serious business.'

'Absolutely,' agreed Diddums, hastily closing the marshmallow bag. 'Ready when you are, boss.'

The Cat looked doubtful. 'All right, but you

must keep up.'

She swept a narrowed eye around the barn.

'Listen out, everyone,' she said at last. 'This is what we're going to do.'

Her voice was cold with menace. 'I have a score to settle tonight.'

2

Horace the Haggis bounded along the bank of the Red Burn without a care in the world. Bagpipes over his shoulder and hair gelled to perfection, he was on his way to Nut Tower, home of Acre Valley's accident-prone inventor, Professor Brian Nut.

Since making Acre Valley his home, Horace had explored far and wide. He knew his way to Ronald Rook's tree, where everyone goes for the best gossip. He knew exactly where Doc Leaf the owl takes his naps (making sure he practised his piping somewhere else).

His best friend Martha Mouse had introduced him to several dozen cousins in Mouse Mountain, whose names he would never remember. He had visited the duck pond to seek out shy little Nobby the newt, who always liked to know what was going on, even if he did dart off at the first sign of trouble.

Horace had also spent hours over at Major Mole's place, being endlessly reminded of how the valour of the Mole Patrol had saved his life during the great Battle of Nettle Farm.

Lately he had struck up a friendship with Professor Nut over at the Secret Loch. The squirrel wanted to learn the bagpipes. Horace, deeply flattered, was on his way to give him his first lesson.

The only place in Acre Valley where Horace never, ever ventured was the farm beyond the deer woods. No way was he going to risk bumping into the haggis hunter Angus McPhee again. There had been no sign of his Cat either since the Battle of Nettle Farm. The thought gave Horace a thrill of pleasure. The Cat With No Name must have forgotten all about him by now.

His favourite place in the valley was Dun Foxin', the home Ferdy Fox shares with Dijon the robin in Daffodil Meadow. They always kept a sprig or two of heather especially for him in a bowl by the window.

'I'll just pop in on my way past, before it gets dark,' he thought. As usual, Horace was feeling peckish.

Ferdy was not at home, but his French chef Dijon opened the door, looking flustered. There was a smell of burning.

'You come at a bad time, *mon ami**. My bramble jam, it ees ruined. I turn away for one moment and – *pouf* – it burns in ze pan.'

They both gazed at the gooey purple mess. A tear dripped along the robin's beak and down his plump breast. 'And I promised Ferdy it would be ready for dinner.'

Horace didn't like jam, but he felt so sorry for Dijon that he offered to help him collect another pan-load of blackberries from the bramble hedge outside. He was about to leave when Dijon begged him to keep an eye on the bubbling mixture, in case it burned again. He just couldn't get away.

'Here, taste this, 'Orace,' twittered the robin

* *mon ami* = my friend

at last, handing him a long, shiny ladle. 'Zis time my jam it ees perfect.'

Reluctantly Horace took the ladle. But as he did, he looked out of the window. He had been here so long that night was falling. The burn was no more than a shadow. He could see the faint outlines of a huge moon.

'Sorry, Dijon,' he mumbled. 'Professor Nut is expecting me. I really must go.'

He reached the door and fled. Behind him he could hear Dijon twittering excitedly, *'Mon cher haggis*, you 'ave forgotten . . .'*

But Horace had no intention of finding out what he had forgotten. He was late enough. Clutching his pipes, he bounded off in the gathering darkness towards the Secret Loch.

* *Mon cher haggis* = My dear haggis

3

High in Acre Valley the door of the barn creaked open. Five shadowy figures slipped out of Nettle Farm and streamed silently into the darkness.

Not one of them gave Mouse Mountain so much as a glance as they slid past. They were after something much tastier tonight.

A huge white ball of moon hung in the sky. Their eyes gleamed in the light of it. Their teeth flashed. The hunt was on.

4

Ronald Rook had news to report. He was hopping from one foot to the other in a state of high excitement.

'It was enormous, I tell you. A monster. A huge, silver, ghostly thing with evil eyes. Sparks flying. As big as a tree, I swear it.'

The animals stared at him. 'Are you sure, Ronald?' Ferdy Fox asked sternly. 'You know how you like to exaggerate.'

'Me? Exaggerate?' The rook turned his back and ruffled his glossy feathers. 'I've never been so insulted in all my life.'

Martha scampered up to him. 'It's not that we don't believe you, Ronald. It just seems a little, well, unlikely.' She giggled. 'Where did you see this, um, monster?'

Ronald hopped round to face them again. 'I was flying back from my singing lesson . . .'

Martha giggled again and Major Mole had a sudden coughing fit. Ronald looked hurt.

'Excuse *me*. I have an extremely fine voice. Just needs some training, that's all. Anyway, I noticed this strange light in the sky.'

'Where was it?' rumbled Doc Leaf. In the darkness the owl's eyes looked even bigger than usual.

'Over by the Secret Loch. I didn't get a very good look because it kept disappearing in and out of the trees. But it was huge and silvery and . . .' Ronald lowered his voice. ' . . . Something else. There were noises.'

'Noises?' snapped Ferdy. 'What kind?'

'Sort of clanking noises, like a tortured soul dragging its chains,' said Ronald dramatically. 'Like a ghost in torment.'

'Pull yourself together, man,' barked Major Mole, waving his torch indignantly. It was almost as big as him. 'When I took on the enemy in the Battle of Nettle Farm, alone and unaided, I didn't go seeing ghosts, I can tell you.'

But Doc Leaf was looking thoughtful. 'Any

of you ever heard of the Acre Valley Ghost Dog?'

'The gh-gh-ghost dog? What is it, Doc?'
asked Martha with a shiver.

'Well, it's an old, old story. My father told
it to stop us young owls flying too far away from
the nest. "Stay close to home," he would say, "or
the Ghost Dog will get you."'

Martha gave a squeak and ran up Ferdy's
tail.

'They say that in life he was a mean and
vicious beast with a cruel master. One day the
dog turned on his master. As a punishment he
was wrapped in chains and thrown in the loch.
Nasty business, really.'

Doc Leaf lowered his voice.
'My dear papa said the dog haunted the valley
ever after. And do you know what he used to tell
us? "When the moon is full and the sky lights
up with fire, beware the Ghost Dog." That's what
he said.'

'Stuff and nonsense,' harrumphed Major
Mole. 'I've never heard such . . .'

He was interrupted by a distant flash.

It streaked across the sky and fell away. The friends looked up, mouths gaping. Martha squealed with fright and burrowed deeper into Ferdy's tail.

As the light died, a strange, tinny sound was carried towards them on the night air. Ronald Rook gave a squawk of terror, flew to the top of the tree and vanished into his nest.

'I told you,' he screeched down at them. 'It's the Ghost Dog of Acre Valley, dragging his chains out of the loch. He's coming to get us all.'

Another spark hit the sky. Another distant clang of metal. Major Mole adjusted his helmet hastily.

'Well, I'd better be going. No sense in hanging around here when I have to, er, er, dust the sitting room.' He disappeared into the ground in a flurry of earth.

Clearing his throat, Doc Leaf said he had a friend to see and flapped off in a hurry.

Ferdy muttered something about jam tarts for dinner and bolted so fast that Martha nearly fell off. However, as they raced along the burn, a thought suddenly struck her. Where was Horace the Haggis? She wondered if she should mention it to Ferdy.

No, he was probably safe at home in his burrow. Just as well. Horace would be terrified if he knew the Ghost Dog was out tonight.

5

Horace had just realised what Dijon was trying to tell him as he rushed out of the house. He had forgotten to give the chef back his ladle.

'Oh well, I'll hand it in tomorrow,' he decided. 'I really can't keep Professor Nut waiting any longer.' He stuck the ladle in his pouch beside the hair gel and hurried on towards the Secret Loch.

It was really dark now. Light from the full moon came and went, as tattered clouds and ribbons of mist drifted across it. Horace found it difficult to see where he was going. He hoped he would be at Nut Tower soon. He was tired and hungry. But it was more than that. There was something creepy about the valley tonight.

As Horace wound his way through the pine wood above the loch, a strange feeling grew on him that he was being . . . watched. Was that an eye blinking among the trees?

He shook himself. Trees don't have eyes.

But then he saw something he could not mistake. Ahead of him a spark of light shot into the sky. He skidded to a halt. And then – what in the world was that? It sounded like chains clattering along the ground.

A shiver crept up Horace's spine. He pulled the ladle out of his pouch and gripped it tightly. It wasn't much of a weapon, but it was better than nothing.

Behind him a dark shape slid silently behind a tree. A tail whisked out of sight.

'I know, I'll make up a song,' Horace thought. 'I'll think about that instead.' He tried his new words to the tune of 'Donald, Where's Your Troosers', the song his mother used to sing to make him laugh:

♪♪ I'm no' very big and I'm awful shy,
I'm trying to be brave but I might just cry.
The dark pine trees they look so high,
But Horace walked on bravely. ♪♪

He shouted the last line to cheer himself up.
Then he wished he hadn't. His voice sounded
very loud.

He looked around. There was nothing
except trees. Nothing at all, except . . . Surely
that really was a pair of eyes?

He rubbed his own eyes and when he looked
again there was nothing. 'I just need some food,'
he muttered. 'I'll be fine after a good dinner.'

Suddenly another flash streaked into the
sky in a burst of light. What was going on?
Horace's fur prickled now with real fear.
Every step was taking him closer to danger.
He knew it.

'What are you, Horace? A haggis or a, er
. . .' He tried to think of a creature less timid
than he was. 'A haggis or a newt?' he finished
triumphantly.

Yes, Nobby the great-crested newt would
have fled long ago. But he was Horace the
Mighty, Horace the Brave. Urging himself
forward he made up another verse, which went
like this:

Horace and the Ghost Dog

♪♪♪ *Strange lights are flashing through the trees,*
Would someone come and help me, please.
What's that knocking? It's my knees.
But Horace walked on bravely. ♪♪

He was proud of that verse and sang it through
a few times. But he was only whispering the last
line now. There was definitely something out
there and it was watching him. He could feel it.

The lights in the sky were almost above him
now. The clanking noises were growing louder.

'Horace walked on bravely,' he quavered,
gripping his ladle tighter.

6

Martha looked shocked. She and Ferdy were outside Dun Foxin'.

'You mean Horace isn't safe at home?' she asked Dijon, who had launched into a long story about burned jam.

'*Non*, he ees gone to the Secret Loch. But, ah, my ladle. My beautiful ladle. What if I never see it again? My heart it will break in two.'

A spark shot into the air from the direction of Pine Hill. The din of clanging metal sounded closer than ever.

'Never mind your precious ladle,' sniffed Martha. 'If the Ghost Dog gets Horace, we may never see him again either.'

At that moment there was a wild eruption of earth and a small helmeted figure shot out of the bank next to them.

'Mole Patrol at your service,' barked Major

Mole. He dusted some earth off his spectacles and swung his torch around with such force that he nearly took off.

'Been keeping my ear to the ground in case this Ghost Dog fellow is getting up to no good. Did I hear that young Horace is heading for the Secret Loch?'

'We've got to find him, Major,' squeaked Martha. 'He doesn't know the danger out there.'

Major Mole fixed them all with a commanding eye. 'Leave it to me, men,' he said, drawing himself up to his full height. Martha glared at him. Men, indeed!

With some difficulty the Major began switching the light on and off. Three quick flashes, then three long ones, then another three short ones.

'Major, what are you doing?' snapped Ferdy impatiently.

'Morse code, my boy. SOS – the emergency signal. Should bring us some reinforcements.'

'I'm scared,' said Martha, burrowing deeper into Ferdy's fur. 'There's something terrible in the air tonight. The Ghost Dog is about – but something else, too. Can't you all feel it?'

7

Horace left the shelter of the pine trees and crept down the slope towards the loch. The lights of Nut Tower twinkled in the distance. Ahead of him lay the water, still and dark.

Suddenly the sky lit up in an enormous flash of white light. A deafening clank of metal sounded right in front of him. There before him was the most terrifying sight he had ever seen.

A giant silver dog, as tall as a man, was lurching towards him. A pair of monster jaws snapped at him with a grind of metal. Its legs clattered as it lunged to attack him.

Horace tried to scramble away, but it was too late. The dog was on top of him, sparks flying as it moved to hold him down.

Horace felt the air being squeezed out of his body. He looked up to see the huge mouth opening wide. It was going to bite him in two.

'We'll see about that,' yelled Horace. 'Am I a haggis or a newt? Take that!'

As the great jaws bore down on him, he thrust Dijon's ladle between them. The dog thrashed about with an almighty clamour of metal, but the ladle held fast. Horace rolled out from under it and prodded himself to see if his bones were still in the right place.

At that moment a small figure bustled out of the darkness towards him. He was wearing a white coat and carrying a box covered in switches and buttons.

'Horace, my dear fellow, I thought you were never coming. I see you've met my latest invention,' said Professor Nut.

30

8

'Professor Nut,' gasped Horace, 'that dog of yours nearly killed me.'

'Did it really?' murmured the professor, shoving his oversized spectacles on to his forehead and peering about. The dog was still crashing around, trying to free its jaws.

'Delighted you haven't come to any harm, dear boy.' He smiled dreamily. 'I've been trying to train the Rufus RP2 to attack for weeks. I was starting to fear he was a bit of a wimp.'

Horace stood up and eyed the professor's box. 'I wonder, Professor, if you could possibly turn him off,' he said politely.

'Oh yes, er, off,' said Professor Nut vaguely. He looked at his control box. 'Now which was the off switch? Hm. Let's try this one.'

He flicked a large switch and they both looked expectantly at the dog. But instead of

31

collapsing, the Rufus RP2 suddenly stood to attention, still facing Horace, its eyes flashing. Horace's heart thudded.

But this time the dog ignored him. Instead it began to clank backwards towards the loch.

'Oh dear, oh dear,' muttered the professor. 'I really must remember to label these switches. Now, if that was reverse, this must be . . .'

Too late. The dog had reached the water's edge. As it scrambled for a foothold, it tried one

final snap of the jaw. Dijon's ladle, horribly bent, flew from its mouth. Then, with one final clank, a shower of sparks and a crazy waving of legs, it toppled into the loch and disappeared. Wisps of mist drifted over the still waters.

For once Professor Nut was speechless. Bushy tail drooping, he gazed sadly at the spot where the dog had disappeared.

'I'm so sorry, Professor,' said Horace. He tried to think of something suitable to say. 'I'm sure he had a long and happy life.'

But the squirrel was not listening. 'If I could just sort out these switches,' he was saying to himself thoughtfully, 'all may not be lost.'

Horace suddenly remembered his bagpipes. He picked them up and gave a quick blow to check they were working. Professor Nut immediately forgot all about the drowned Rufus.

'My dear boy, you brought the pipes. Excellent. Do let me have a look.'

'What? Now?' gulped Horace, thinking of the promised meal at Nut Tower.

'No time like the present,' beamed Professor Nut.

 **9**

Horace's friends were making their way through the pine woods towards the Secret Loch. The SOS signal had alerted everyone.

Ferdy was carrying Martha between his ears and Major Mole on his back. A newt clung to his tail. Ronald Rook hovered overhead, trying to appear braver than he felt. Doc Leaf, wondering what a bite from a ghost would look like, was clutching his first aid case.

Stacey and Tracey Magpie were there too, looking glum. Stacey had tweeted:

S **Stacey Magpie** @StaceEmag
Wicked lights lol #timeforfun

And they had both rushed over expecting a party. Tracey still thought The Ghost Dog was an indie band.

Dijon had not stopped grumbling about his ladle. Martha kept telling him to shut up.

'Listen, everyone!' hushed Ferdy suddenly.

'Listen to what?' croaked Ronald.

'Nothing,' said Ferdy. 'That's the point. Nothing. It's all gone quiet.'

Martha gave a tiny sob. 'Does that mean the Ghost Dog's eaten Horace?'

'Let's go back,' whispered Nobby, cowering deeper inside Ferdy's tail. He was wishing he had never left the duck pond.

'Good idea,' agreed Ronald. 'He'll be after us next.'

'NO!' yelled Martha Mouse in the loudest squeak she had ever summoned. Nobby got such a fright he nearly fell off. 'We are not going back till we find Horace. DO YOU ALL HEAR ME? I don't care who eats us.'

'I do,' sighed Nobby the newt, to no one in particular.

10

At the edge of the loch Professor Nut was turning an interesting shade of purple. He blew again down the tallest of Horace's pipes. Still nothing happened.

'Wrong pipe, Professor,' Horace chuckled. 'You blow through the little one to fill the bag with air.'

Professor Nut tried the wrong pipes one after another, nearly blowing himself up in the effort to get a note.

It was then that Horace saw it. Something was creeping down the slope towards him. It was no mechanical dog this time. The smile froze on his lips.

'P-P-Professor, look!' whispered Horace. 'Not now, Horace,' said Professor Nut, who had somehow managed to wind the bag round his neck. 'I'm just finding the right end.'

Horace and the Ghost Dog

Horace's mouth opened, but no sound emerged.
A set of glittering yellow eyes seemed to be
floating down the slope in the darkness. He felt
his legs turning to jelly.

Horace and the Ghost Dog

The creature had ten eyes. Five tails. Twenty legs. Teeth gleaming with malice.

'Professor, it's a monster,' hissed Horace in panic. 'A real monster.'

'What's that, dear boy?' muttered the professor. 'I'll be with you in a jiffy. Almost got this thing figured out.'

The eyes advanced. Horace took a step backwards.

The dark tails waved menacingly. Horace took another step backwards – and tripped over something behind him. He sat down hard. It was the professor's control box. One of the pointy switches was sticking right into him. Horace leaped off again, and as he did the switch moved.

Deep under the dark waters of the loch, something stirred.

'Now, let me see,' Professor Nut was murmuring. 'I do believe I've got it this time.' He tucked the bag under his arm and put a small pipe to his mouth.

Horace didn't know what to do. The shadowy monster had turned into lots of separate shapes now, and he saw with a terrible shudder that each one, every single one, was . . . A CAT.

They had fanned out and were creeping towards him now from all sides, fangs and claws horribly lit by the moonlight. Horace knew at once there was no escape.

As the professor practised some deep breaths, still blissfully unaware of the danger, Horace braced himself. He spotted the bent ladle at his feet and picked it up. He was a haggis, not a newt. He would not go down without a fight.

'Attack!' screamed a voice that made Horace's blood run cold. He knew that voice. He knew in that moment that he was finished.

Behind his back a silvery shape broke the surface of the water.

11

'Horace walked on bravely!' the terrified haggis shouted at his attackers. Well, it was worth a try. To his utter astonishment the five cats skidded to a halt just in front of him.

'Aha! HORACE WALKED ON BRAVELY!' he roared at them again, thrilled at the effect his words seemed to be having.

Now the cats' fur was standing on end. They were pointing at him, scrambling backwards, falling over each other in terror. This was brilliant.

Then Horace heard a familiar clanking. He whirled around and gasped. Right behind him the Rufus RP2 was heaving itself out of the loch. Dripping weeds and water, its huge body gleaming spookily in the moonlight, it clattered past him towards the cowering cats.

'Dog!' yowled one. 'Ghost!' screamed another. 'Mummy!' sobbed the large one at the back.

The Cat With No Name tried to rally her troops. 'Cowards,' she screeched. 'Don't give in. You can still get him.'

At that moment Professor Nut finally managed his first blow of the pipes. A blood-curdling wail sounded around the loch. It seemed to be coming from the very mouth of the dog itself, as it lurched drunkenly towards the cats.

The effect on McPhee's Cat was electric. 'Over to you, Skull,' she muttered hastily, and before the others could gather their wits she was off, streaking back up the slope towards the trees.

'Do your own hunting next time,' spat Skull, and made off behind her.

The professor was enjoying himself. Pumping up the bag again, he sent another ghostly moan into the night.

With a yowl of terror, the other cats turned tail. Diddums got such a fright that she dropped what she was carrying. She tore up the hill behind the others and disappeared into the dark wood.

Professor Nut stopped blowing. 'So that's how you do it,' he said breathlessly. 'Hard work, eh, but well worth the effort. Ah, Horace, I see you managed to get Rufus moving again. Which switch was it, then?'

Horace was standing still, completely stunned. 'I don't know, Professor. I've been a little busy.'

At that moment another commotion made them both look up. More shapes were streaming out of the wood, where the cats had disappeared.

Horace clutched the professor in alarm. His heart started to thump all over again.

The shapes hurtled down the hill. As they came closer, urgent voices could be heard. One rose above all the others.

'I tell you, I don't care if those cats do come back for me. We've got to save him from the Ghost Dog.'

Horace recognised the gutsy squeak of Martha Mouse and sagged with relief. Beside him Professor Nut dithered on, gazing at the box of switches doubtfully. 'Well, here goes.'

He pushed a small red button. Immediately the giant dog's legs buckled, and with an ear-splitting clang and a final spray of sparks, it collapsed on the ground in a heap of metal.

'Good dog, Rufus,' said the professor fondly.

12

Soon the friends were together in Nut Tower around a crackling pinecone fire. The professor was busy outlining his plans for an army of robot dogs to protect the valley from The Cat With No Name and her gang.

'What a pity I've never had a chance to try Rufus out on real cats,' he sighed.

Horace, tucking into his third helping of heather hotpot, winked at the others. He had told them how Rufus had scared off his attackers without the squirrel even noticing. They all shared a secret smile. Trust Professor Nut to miss everything.

'But the real news tonight,' the squirrel said proudly, 'is that I have learned to play the bagpipes.'

A loud groan went round the room. 'Not two of you,' moaned Doc Leaf, putting his head in his wings.

'Yes, I intend to make myself a set of pipes right away,' said Professor Nut. 'But now, everyone, how about some hot chocolate?'

'And I 'ave just ze thing to eat with it,' twittered Dijon.

Horace went pale. Not more jam.

'I found zis lying on ze grass on the way here.' The robin let a large pink bag drop from his beak. Its contents spilled out in a cascade of soft, powdery cubes.

'Marshmallows!' squealed Martha, clapping her hands in delight. 'My favourite.'

Late into the night the friends sat around the fire toasting marshmallows, drinking chocolate and singing the songs of the valley.

Stacey tweeted happily:

Horace and the Ghost Dog

And Tracey posted a sneaky photo on Facebook of Major Mole with his glasses on upside down.

In a loud and none too tuneful voice, Ronald added a new verse to Horace's song:

♪♪ *Now dogs may come and cats may go,*
But Prof will give a mighty blow,
And friends arrive to fight the foe,
When Horace walks on bravely. ♪♪

Everyone joined in, and they sang until the fire had burned low and all the heads were nodding sleepily. All except Dijon's.

He fluttered on to Horace's shoulder. 'I 'ave a question for you, 'Orace. It ees very important.'

Dijon was looking wide awake – and very stern. 'Tell me zis, *mon ami*. Where is my beautiful ladle?'

Horace swallowed. He thought about the bent and twisted stick of metal he had brandished at the cats.

'I'll, er, tell you tomorrow, Dijon,' said Horace the Haggis.

The End